THE CHILDREN OF NOISY VILLAGE

My name is Lisa and I am a girl as you can tell by my name. I am nine years old, but I'll soon be ten. Sometimes my mother says, "You're Mommy's big girl and you can dry the dishes today."

But other times Karl and Bill—they're my brothers—say, "We don't want any little girls playing Indians with us. You're too little."

So I wonder which I am, big or little. When some people think you're big and some people think you're little, maybe that means you're just the right size.

Join highly-acclaimed storyteller Astrid Lindgren on a visit to the three Swedish "neighboring farms that everybody calls 'noisy village' because six high-spirited nine-to-eleven-year-olds live there," and share with them a year filled with all of the warmth and tradition of life in the Swedish countryside.

By the Same Author

THE BROTHERS LIONHEART
MIO MY SON
MISCHIEVOUS MEG
PIPPI GOES ON BOARD
PIPPI LONGSTOCKING
PIPPI IN THE SOUTH SEAS
RASMUS AND THE VAGABOND
RONIA, THE ROBBER'S DAUGHTER

THE CHILDREN OF NOISY VILLAGE

by *Astrid Lindgren*

Illustrated by Ilon Wikland
Translated by Florence Lamborn

SCHOLASTIC INC.

New York   Toronto   London   Auckland   Sydney

ISBN 0-590-44760-2

Copyright © 1961 by Astrid Lindgren.
Translation copyright © 1962 by Viking Penguin.
Renewed 1990 by Viking Penguin, a division of Penguin Books USA, Inc.
All rights reserved. Published by Scholastic Inc., 730 Broadway, New York, NY 10003, by arrangement with Puffin Books, a division of Penguin Books USA Inc.

12 11 10 9 8 7 6 5 4 3 2 1   1 2 3 4 5 6/9

Printed in the U.S.A.   42

First Scholastic printing, January 1991

CONTENTS

· 6 · CONTENTS

THE CHILDREN OF NOISY VILLAGE

1 THE CHILDREN OF NOISY VILLAGE

MY NAME is Lisa, and I am a girl, as you can tell by my name. I am nine years old, but I'll soon be ten.

Sometimes my mother says, "You're Mommy's big girl and you can dry the dishes today."

But other times Karl and Bill—they're my brothers—say, "We don't want any little girls playing Indians with us. You're too little."

So I wonder which I am, big or little. When some people think you're big and some think you're little, maybe that means you're just the right size.

Karl is eleven years old and Bill is ten. Karl is awfully strong and can run faster than I can, but I can run just as fast as Bill. Sometimes, when the boys don't want me to play with them, Karl holds me while Bill runs a little way to get a head start on me. Then when Karl lets me go he runs away from me as easily as anything. It's too bad that I don't have any sisters, because boys are such a nuisance.

We live on a farm called Middle Farm, because it's right between two other farms. The others are called North Farm and South Farm, and all three of them are in a row like this:

They really don't look exactly like this because I can't draw very well. Everybody calls the farms Noisy Village because there are so many children around, making so much noise all the time.

A boy named Olaf lives at South Farm. He has a little sister named Kerstin who is a year and a half old. Olaf plays with Karl and Bill. He is ten years old and runs fast too.

At North Farm there are two girls and no boys. What luck! Britta is eleven years old, and Anna is just my age. I like them both very much. Well, maybe I like Anna just a little bit more.

That's all the children there are in Noisy Village.

2 BROTHERS ARE A NUISANCE!

KARL and Bill and I used to sleep in the same room. It was the right gable-room which is next to the attic. But now I live in the left gable-room, which Grandmother used to have. I'll tell you more about that later.

Sometimes it's a lot of fun to live in the same room as your brothers, but only sometimes. One thing that was fun was when we lay in bed at night and told each other ghost stories. But it was scary too. Karl told such awful ghost stories and I was so scared that I had to lie under the blanket a long, long time afterward. Bill doesn't tell ghost stories; he only talks about the adventures that he's going to have when he grows up. Then he is going to America where the Indians live and become an Indian chief.

One night when Karl had told an awful story about a ghost who went around in a house and moved all the furniture, I was so scared that I thought I would die. It was almost dark in the room, and my bed stood very far away from the boys'. All of a sudden one of the chairs started jumping back and forth. I thought it was the ghost, who had come to our house too and was moving our furniture, and I yelled as loud as I could. Then I heard them giggling over in their beds. And do you know what they had done? They had tied strings to the chair and were pulling it back and forth to make it jump. It's just like them. I got mad at first, but then I couldn't help laughing.

When you sleep in the same room as your brothers and they are bigger than you are, you're never allowed to decide anything. For one thing, it was always Karl who decided when the light should be turned out at night. When I wanted to read, Karl wanted to turn out the light and tell ghost stories. When I wanted to sleep, Karl and Bill left the light on to play Old Maid.

Karl could turn out the light whenever he wanted to from his bed. He had put a piece of cardboard around the light switch, and to the cardboard he had fastened a string that stretched to his bed. It's quite a clever arrangement, but I can't really describe it because I'm not going to be one of those whirl-around-trundlebolt-engineers. I don't know what that is, but Karl says it's something very fancy that he's going to be when he grows up, and you have to be able to put pieces of cardboard around light switches to become one.

Bill has always said he's going to be an Indian chief, but the other day I heard him say that he was going to be an engineer on a train, so perhaps he's changed his mind. I don't quite know what I'm going to be, but probably a mother, because I like little babies. I have six dolls that are my children. Soon I'll be too big to play with dolls. My, it's going to be sad to get that big!

The prettiest doll I ever had was called Bella, but I gave her away some time ago to a little girl who was very sick. Bella had blue eyes and blond curly hair. She lay in her bed with a pink blanket and sheets that Mommy had made. One day, when I was going to lift Bella out of bed, I found that she had a mustache and a beard. Karl and Bill had painted them on with a piece of charcoal. So you see some of the reasons that I'm very glad I don't sleep in their room any more.

Middle Farm and South Farm are terribly close together, and when you look out of Karl's and Bill's window you can see right into Olaf's room. Daddy thinks that the people who built the houses should have left a little more room between. But Bill and Olaf think they're just fine the way they are. There is a fence between Middle Farm and South Farm, and beside the fence is a huge linden tree. Its branches stretch from Karl's and Bill's window all the way to Olaf's. When the boys want to call on one another they just climb right through the tree. This is much faster than to run down the stairs, out through the gate, in through the next gate, and up the stairs. Once our daddy and Olaf's daddy wanted to cut down the tree because it made the rooms so dark. But the boys nagged so terribly and begged them so hard not to do it that they left it standing. And it still stands there.

3 MY NICEST BIRTHDAY

I THINK that the nicest days of the whole year are Christmas and my birthday. But my very nicest birthday was when I was seven years old. This is what happened.

I woke up very early. I lived in Karl's and Bill's room then, and they were still sleeping. I had a squeaky bed, so I turned over many times to make it squeak so much that they would wake up. When you have a birthday you have to pretend to be sleeping until someone brings you hot chocolate in bed, so I couldn't call them, and there they lay, sleeping, instead of getting up to get things ready. Finally, after I had made my bed squeak and squeak, Bill sat up and scratched his head. Then he woke Karl, and the two of them sneaked out into the attic and down the stairs. I could hear Mommy clattering with the cups and saucers down in the kitchen, and I was so excited I could hardly lie still.

At last I heard steps on the stairs. I closed my eyes as tightly as I could, and then, bang, the door opened and there stood Mommy and Daddy, Karl, Bill, and Agda, our maid. Mommy carried a tray with a cup of chocolate on it. There was also a vase with flowers and a large cake with sugar and currants which Agda had baked. She had written "Lisa 7 years old" in white frosting. But there weren't any presents anywhere, so I began to think it was a pretty strange birthday. Then Daddy said, "Drink your chocolate, and then we'll see if we can't find a present for you."

Then I knew they had a surprise for me, so I swallowed the chocolate as fast as I could. Mommy blindfolded me with a towel, and Daddy twirled me around and around before he carried me some place that I couldn't see. I could hear Karl and Bill running beside me. I could feel it too, because they pinched my toes now and then and said, "Guess where you are!"

Daddy carried me down the stairs and all around some more. For a while I could tell that we were outdoors, and

then we went up some stairs again. When Mommy took
away the towel, we were in a room that I had never seen

before—at least I didn't think I had seen it. But when I happened to look out of the window, I could see the gable of North Farm a little farther away, and in the window of the gable were Britta and Anna waving to me. Then I understood that I was in Grandmother's old room and that Daddy had walked the long way round just to confuse me.

When Grandmother moved to Aunt Frida's, Mommy put her loom and large piles of rag carpets in that room. Now all those things were gone. It was such a fine room that I thought there must have been a magician there. Mommy said that there had been a magician all right, and Daddy was it—he'd made me this room for my birthday present. I was so happy that I laughed and jumped up and down and thought it was the best birthday present I had ever had.

Daddy said that Mommy had made magic too. She had made the curtains, and Daddy had put up the pretty wallpaper, which had lots of tiny little bouquets of flowers. Daddy had stayed down in the workshop at night to make a chest of drawers and a round table and a bookshelf and three chairs. Mommy had made the rag carpets with red and yellow and green and black stripes. I had seen her weaving them during the winter but I had never thought they were for me. I had seen Daddy make the furniture too. But he is always making furniture for people who can't make their own, so I never guessed it was for me either.

Karl and Bill carried my bed across the attic and into my new room, and Karl said, "But we'll still come in to see you at night and tell ghost stories."

The first thing I did was to run back into the boys' room to get my dolls. I had four little dolls and three big ones, and I made a room in the bookshelf for the little dolls.

First I put a piece of red cloth down as a carpet, then I arranged my pretty dolls' chairs and table that Grandmother had given me, and then I placed the little dolls' beds on the shelf and put the little dolls themselves in the beds. Now they had a room of their own too, just like me, although it wasn't their birthday. I put Bella's large doll's bed in a corner right next to my own bed, and the doll-carriage that Hansel and Gretel slept in over in another corner. My, how beautiful my room looked!

I ran back again into Karl's and Bill's room and got all my boxes and things that I had in their chest of drawers, and Bill said, "Good! Now I'll have a little more room for my birds' eggs!"

I have thirteen books of my own. I put them in the bookshelf with my boxes of bookmarks. We trade bookmarks in school, but I have twenty that I wouldn't give up for anything at all. The finest one is a large angel with a pink dress and golden wings. There was room for just everything in my bookshelf. It was certainly a nice day when I got my own room.

4 MORE FUN ON MY BIRTHDAY

I HAD still more fun that day. In the afternoon I had a juice party for all the children in Noisy Village. There was just room enough for the six of us around the new round table in my own room. We had raspberry juice and slices of cake with "Lisa 7 years old" on it, and two other kinds of cake that Agda had also baked. Britta and Anna and Olaf brought me presents. Britta and Anna gave me a story book, and Olaf gave me a chocolate bar. He sat down next to me, and my brothers started teasing us.

"Boyfriend and girlfriend, boyfriend and girlfriend!"

They say that just because Olaf is not one of those silly boys who won't play with girls. He doesn't care if Karl and Bill do tease him; he plays with both boys and girls anyway. Karl and Bill want to play with girls too, although they pretend they don't. When there are only six children in a village, all the boys and girls have to play together, because almost all games are more fun with six than with only three.

After a while the boys went to look at Bill's birds' eggs, and Britta and Anna and I played with my dolls.

I had a long, long string in my pocket. When I happened to pull it out and saw how long it was, I thought of a way to have fun with it. If we got another string just as long and tied them together, they would probably reach all the way to Britta's and Anna's window at North Farm. And then we could send letters to each other on it in a little basket. My, how we hurried to see if it would work! And it did.

At first we couldn't figure out how to slide the basket back and forth along the string. But Britta, who is clever, thought of a way. I got another very, very, *very* long piece of string from our kitchen, and Anna and Britta ran home and got two more long pieces. Anna took theirs up to their bedroom window and dropped the ends of both pieces down to Britta, who stood below. I dangled my strings down from my window so Britta could reach them when she came across, holding the ends of Anna's. I tossed the little basket to her, and she tied one of my strings and one of Anna's to the handle. Then she slipped the ends of the other two strings through the handle and tied them in a tight knot. When Anna and I pulled our ends of the strings, up came the basket swinging on the straight line, and each of us tied the end of that to the back of a chair inside the room. With the other strings we could make the basket ride back and forth quite easily. It was great fun!

We sat in our windows for a long while, sending letters to each other. First we only wrote: "How are you? I am well." But afterward we pretended that we were princesses who were locked up in two castles and couldn't get out because there were dragons who guarded us. Britta and Anna wrote to me: "Our dragon is so awfully scary. Is yours? Princess Britta and Princess Anna."

And I answered: "Yes, my dragon is awfully scary too. He bites me if I try to get out. How nice that we can, at least, write to each other. Princess Lisa."

After a while Mommy called and asked me to run an errand, and while I was away Karl and Bill and Olaf came into my room and saw the letters, so Karl sent a letter in the basket which said: "Princess Lisa has gone out to lunch, but there are lots of princes here. Prince Karl Alexander Napoleum."

Britta and Anna thought that was a silly letter.

It's good that my room is on the side of our house that faces North Farm, because we still send letters to each other, Britta, Anna, and I. In the winter, when it's dark, it doesn't work as well. Then we blink at each other with flashlights instead. If I blink three times it means: "Come over right away! I have something to tell you."

Mommy has said that I have to keep my room nice and neat. I do the best I can. Sometimes I have general housecleaning. Then I throw all the rag carpets out through the window, and Agda helps me to beat them. I polish my door-handle and dust all my furniture and put fresh flowers in my vase and make up the doll-bed and doll-carriage. When I forget to clean my room Mommy calls me a draggletail.

5 HOW OLAF GOT HIS DOG

OLAF doesn't have any brothers or sisters old enough to play with him, but he has a dog named Skip. Now I am going to tell you how Olaf got Skip, just as he told it to us.

Halfway between Noisy Village and the real village there lives a shoemaker whose name is Kind. His name is Kind, but he *isn't* kind, not the least bit. He never has our shoes ready when we go to pick them up, even if he has promised us ever so many times.

He owned Skip before Olaf, but he was never kind to Skip, who was the meanest dog in the whole parish. He always had to be tied to his doghouse, and every time we took shoes to Mr. Kind, Skip rushed out of his house and barked. We were so scared of Skip that we never dared go near him. We were scared of the shoemaker too, because he was always so cross and because he said, "Youngsters are a wild lot who should get spanked every day." Skip got spanked often too, although he was a dog and not a youngster. And Mr. Kind forgot to feed Skip most of the time.

When Skip lived with the shoemaker, I thought he was ugly and mean. He was dirty and shaggy and he growled or barked all the time, but now I think he is a nice and pretty dog. Olaf has made him nice because he is so nice himself.

One day when Olaf went to the shoemaker with his shoes, Skip rushed out, as usual, and barked and looked as if he wanted to bite Olaf. Olaf stopped and talked to him. He said, "You are a nice dog and you shouldn't bark like that." Of course he kept his distance so Skip couldn't get near enough to bite him, but Skip didn't act like a nice dog at all and looked just as surly as ever.

When Olaf came back a few days later to get his shoes, he brought along a meat-bone for Skip. Skip barked and growled, but he was so hungry that he started gnawing the bone. All the time he was eating, Olaf stood there and told him that he was a nice dog and a good dog.

Olaf's shoes weren't ready and he had to go back and ask for them several times, and every time he brought something good for Skip. Then one day Skip didn't growl at Olaf but just barked the way dogs do when they see someone they like. So Olaf went over and patted him on the head, and Skip licked his hand.

One day not long after that the shoemaker tripped and sprained his ankle. Of course he didn't care whether Skip got any food or not. Olaf felt so sorry for Skip that he went in and asked Mr. Kind if he could take care of him while Mr. Kind was laid up with his sore foot.

Mr. Kind said, "Ha, that would be a fine mess. He'd jump at your throat as soon as you got near him."

But Olaf went out to Skip and patted him, and the shoemaker limped over to the window and watched. And then he said that Olaf could take care of Skip as long as he couldn't do it himself.

First Olaf cleaned Skip's doghouse, put new straw on the floor, cleaned his water dish, and filled it with fresh water. Then he gave him a lot of food. After that he took him for a long walk all the way home to Noisy Village, and Skip jumped and yelped with joy, for he had been tied up a long time and was tired of it. Every day, as long as Mr. Kind had to take care of his sore ankle, Olaf took Skip out for a run. We ran with them too, but Skip liked Olaf best. No one else could hold his leash, because he growled.

When the shoemaker's ankle got well he said to Olaf, "Now we've had enough of this nonsense. The dog is a watchdog and should stay in his doghouse."

Skip thought he was going for a walk with Olaf that day as usual, and when Olaf left without him he whined and sounded very sad. Olaf too was sad for days and days. Finally his father couldn't stand to see him so unhappy, so he bought Skip from Mr. Kind and gave him to Olaf. All of us children in Noisy Village went over to Olaf's house and watched while Olaf gave Skip a bath in their laundry room. We helped a little. When Skip had been bathed and dried and combed, he looked like a different dog.

Now he is never angry and never needs to walk on a leash. He sleeps every night under Olaf's bed, and when the whole crowd of us Noisy Village children come home from school, Skip comes to meet Olaf and carries his school bag. But he will never go as far as Mr. Kind's house. Perhaps he's afraid that Mr. Kind will come out and take him back.

6 A GRANDFATHER IS FUN, TOO

I'T'S FUN to have an animal of your very own. I'd like to have a dog like Olaf's, but I don't. We have all sorts of other animals here in Noisy Village, horses and cows and calves and pigs and sheep. And Mommy has lots of chickens. We call our place the Noisy Village Chicken Farm, and Mommy sends eggs to people who want chicks. One of the horses, whose name is Ajax, is mine. But still, he isn't *really* mine, the way Skip is Olaf's. I have rabbits that are really my own. They live in a cage that Daddy made, and every day I give them grass and dandelion leaves. In the winter I put their cage in the barn. They have lots of babies, and I have sold dozens of them to Bill and Olaf. Bill kept rabbits too for a while, but he soon got tired of them. He gets tired of everything except his birds' eggs.

In our garden there is an old tree that we call the Owl Tree because some owls live in it. One day Bill climbed up in the owl tree and took one egg out of the nest. There were still three left. Bill blew out the inside of the egg and put it in the chest of drawers with his other birds' eggs. But then he got the idea that he would play a joke on the mama owl, so he climbed up to the nest and put a chicken egg there instead. Wasn't it strange that the mama owl couldn't tell the difference? But she didn't. She kept sitting on the eggs until one day there were three baby owls and one baby chick in the nest. How surprised the mama owl must have been when she saw that one of her babies looked like a little yellow ball! Bill was afraid that the mama owl wouldn't like the chick, so he took it away.

"Anyway, it's my chick," he said. He let it out among Mommy's chicks with a red ribbon around its leg so that he would be able to tell it apart. He called it Albert. When Albert grew up, though, he didn't turn into a rooster but a hen. Then Bill changed Albert's name to Albertina. Now Albertina is a big hen, and when Bill eats eggs he says, "I bet Albertina has laid this egg just for me."

Albertina flies and flaps her wings more than any of the other hens. Bill says that's probably because she was born in an owl's nest.

Once Karl thought that he too would have some animals of his own. So he put three traps in the pigsty and caught sixteen large rats that he locked up in a barrel. Then he painted a large sign and put it on the barrel: "The Noisy Village Rat Farm." But in the night the rats got out of the barrel and ran away, so the rat farm wasn't a very good business.

"Why did you want to have a rat farm in the first place?" Britta asked. "Rats don't lay eggs."

"It would have been fun to have a rat farm anyway. Can't you understand that?" said Karl, who was upset because the rats had run away.

Britta and Anna don't have a dog, or rabbits, or any other animals of their own. But they do have a grandfather. He's the nicest grandfather in the whole world, I'm sure of that. All the children in Noisy Village call him Grandfather, although he isn't ours, but Britta's and Anna's.

He lives in a room on the top floor at North Farm. It's such a nice room and such a nice grandfather that we all go there when we have nothing else to do.

Grandfather sits in a rocking chair and he has a long white beard, just like Santa Claus. His eyes are so weak that he can hardly see anything. He can't read any books or newspapers, but that doesn't matter, because he knows everything in the books anyway. He tells us stories from the Bible and about how things were in the olden times when he was a little boy.

We read the newspaper to him, Britta and Anna and I,
about who has died, and who's had his fiftieth birthday,

and all the accidents and advertisements and everything. If it says in the paper that some building has been struck by lightning, Grandfather can tell us about twenty different places at least that were struck by lightning in olden times. If the paper says that someone has been gored to death by a bull, Grandfather tells us about all the people that he has known who have been chased by angry bulls. This way it takes quite a long time to read the whole paper. Sometimes the boys read to Grandfather. But he likes it better when Britta and Anna and I do it because the boys read carelessly and skip some of the ads and small bits of news.

Grandfather has a tool box in his closet which he lets the boys use, and even though he can't see he helps them to make boats and all kinds of things. When they are making lead soldiers, it's always Grandfather who lets them melt lead in his fireplace.

Grandfather always has a box of apples in his closet—well, not always, of course, but when it's the season that you can have apples. Then he gives us an apple every time we go to see him. Often he has barley-sugar in a bag in his corner cupboard too, so sometimes he gives us both apples and barley-sugar.

Grandfather has geraniums growing on his window sills, and he takes very good care of them even if he is almost blind. He talks as if they were people. On the walls in Grandfather's room there are pretty pictures, two that I like especially well. One shows Jonah in the stomach of the whale, and the other shows a snake that has escaped from a zoo and is squeezing a man to death. Maybe they're not exactly *pretty*, but they're scary and exciting.

When the weather is nice Grandfather goes out for a walk. He has a cane to feel his way along. In the summer he usually sits under a big elm tree on the lawn at North Farm. There he sits in the sunshine, and from time to time he sighs and says, "My, oh my!"

When we ask him why he says "My, oh my," Grandfather says it's because he's thinking about when he was young. That must have been an awfully long time ago. I just love Grandfather! I would rather have him than a dog.

7 WE THINK WE'LL RUN AWAY

THERE is nobody I like to play with as much as Anna. We have many pretend-games that only she and I know about. Sometimes we pretend that we are two ladies calling on each other. Anna's name is Mrs. Bergman, and my name is Mrs. Larsson. And sometimes we pretend that Mrs. Bergman and Mrs. Larsson have a quarrel. Then Anna says,

WE THINK WE'LL RUN AWAY · 37 ·

"Mrs. Larsson, you can just go home with your impossible brats!"

It's my dolls that she calls "impossible brats." And then I say, "I think it's your brats that are impossible, Mrs. Bergman!"

But then we become friends again and pretend to go shopping for silk and velvet and candy which we buy with pretend-money that we make up in Grandfather's room. We don't want Karl and the others to hear how we pretend, because they'll laugh at us. If Grandfather hears us it doesn't matter, because he pretends himself sometimes, and we often buy something from him with our pretend-money.

When it rains Anna and I often sit in Grandfather's room and read the paper to him. His father and mother both died when he was a little boy, and he had to live with people who weren't nice to him at all. He had to work hard, although he was very little, and he got spanked so often and got so little to eat that finally he got tired of the whole thing and ran away. And you can't imagine how many funny and exciting adventures he had before he finally came to nice people he could stay with.

One rainy day when Anna and I were in Grandfather's room and had finished reading the paper, Anna said, "Grandfather, tell us about the time you ran away."

"My goodness," said Grandfather, "you've already heard about that so many times."

But we coaxed him to tell about it once more, so he did. Afterward Anna said, "It must be fun to run away. I'd like to myself."

"Yes, but first you have to have some mean people to run away from," I said.

"That wouldn't be necessary," said Anna. "Couldn't you run away anyway? Just a little bit! And then come back again?"

"Oh, yes, let's do that," I said.

"What do you say, Grandfather?" said Anna. "Do you think we can do it?"

Grandfather said sure, we could always run away a little bit. So we decided we would. We had to do it at night, of course, so nobody would know about it. We asked Grandfather not to tell anyone, and he promised he wouldn't.

I always have such a hard time keeping awake at night, I just didn't know how I would keep from going to sleep before it was time to run away. But Anna said, "You can go on to sleep. We'll tie a string around your big toe and hang the string out of the window. Then I'll come and pull it, and you'll wake up."

Anna said that she was going to put prickly juniper twigs in her bed, and that way she thought that she would be able to stay awake until everyone else had gone to sleep.

We asked Grandfather what you should take with you when you ran away. He said that you should take some food, and a little money if you had any. We were going to run away that night, so we had an awful time getting everything together. I asked Mommy for some sandwiches, and she said, "What? Are you hungry again already? We've just finished supper."

I couldn't tell her what I wanted the sandwiches for, so I didn't say anything. When I got to my room I took some coins out of my money bank and put them under my pillow. And then I looked for a long string to tie around my big toe.

In the evening all of us children played ball, and when it was finally time to go to bed Anna and I winked at each other and whispered, "At ten-thirty!"

I gave Mommy and Daddy very big hugs when I said goodnight because I thought I wouldn't see them for a long time. And when Mommy said, "Tomorrow my little girl and I are going to pick currants," I felt terribly sorry for Mommy because she wouldn't have any little girl tomorrow.

I went up to my room and tied the string to my big toe and let it out through the window. Then I crept into bed and thought I should hurry up and sleep a little so I wouldn't be so tired when I was running away.

Usually I go to sleep as soon as I put my head on the pillow, but this time I just couldn't. I tried as hard as I could, but every time I moved, the string cut into my toe.

And then I thought about what Mommy would say when she came into my room the next morning and found the bed empty. I felt so sorry for her that I started to cry and I cried a long, long time.

All of a sudden I woke up. My big toe felt funny, and at first I couldn't understand why. Then I remembered. Somebody was pulling the string.

"Yes, Anna, I'm coming," I cried and jumped out of bed and ran to the window. Then I saw that it was broad daylight! Karl was standing below my window and tugging at the string.

"Ouch, ouch!" I cried. "Stop it!"

But he kept on pulling.

"Can't you stop it!" I said.

"Why?" asked Karl.

"Because the string is fastened to my big toe!"

Then Karl laughed and said, "What a funny fish I have caught!"

He wanted to know why the string was tied to my toe, but I didn't stop to explain it to him. I ran over to North Farm because I thought Anna must have run away alone. Britta was sitting on the steps, playing with Sessan, her favorite doll.

"Where is Anna?" I asked.

"Still in bed," said Britta.

So I went up to the girls' room, and there Anna lay. She was snoring. I tried to tie the string to her big toe, but she woke up.

"Oh," she said. "What time is it?"

And when I told her it was eight o'clock in the morning, she didn't say anything for a long time. Then she said, "People who can't sleep at night should lie on juniper twigs. You can't imagine how sleepy it makes you."

Then we went up to Grandfather's room to read the paper. He was surprised when we skipped in through his door, and he said, "What are you doing here? Haven't you run away?"

"Some other time," we said.

8 WALKING HOME
FROM SCHOOL

WE ALWAYS have lots of fun when we walk home from school. It's a long walk, because the school is all the way over in the big village. We talk about everything that has happened at school, and we tell each other stories. We also talk about what we're going to do when we grow up, and things like that. Sometimes we sit down by the side of the road to rest, sometimes we climb trees, and sometimes we walk on top of the fence so the walk won't be so dull.

Mommy says she can't understand why it takes more than twice as long to walk home as it does to walk to school. I don't understand it either. But it just can't be helped.

One day last spring, when we came home extra late, Mommy said to me, "Now tell me just exactly what you did on your way home."

So I did. And this is what had happened.

First we went to the store and bought barley-sugar for Grandfather. We wanted to taste a little, but we knew that we shouldn't. Britta put the candy in her schoolbag and said, "If all six of us tasted the barley-sugar, there wouldn't be any left in the bag for Grandfather."

"That would never do," said Karl. "We'd better hurry home with it before something happens."

We started off, but Bill was still thinking about the barley-sugar.

"I wish I had a lot of money!" he said. "I'd spend it all on candy."

"Yes, but it so happens that you don't have any money," said Anna.

"No, but what if I happened to find some?" said Bill.

"You couldn't happen to find anything," said Britta, "because you're always walking with your nose in the air. If you looked at the ground from time to time, maybe you would find something."

So Bill started to look at the ground. And sure enough he had not walked more than fifty yards before he found a krona. We thought maybe there were fairies who can hear what you wish and who walk around leaving money on the road. This krona was lying right in the road, where it forks off to Noisy Village.

At first Bill just stood still, staring at the krona as if he thought it was a joke. But then he picked it up and ran back to the store to buy candy, just as he had said he would. We waited at the fork, and when he came back we all got candy.

"Just think how easy it is to find money," said Bill. "My, what piles of money I've been missing."

After that we all walked along staring at the ground. Karl said, "I wish I had a krona!"

He must have thought the fairy would give him a krona too. But he didn't find anything at all, so he said, "I wish I had ten ore!"

But he didn't even find that much. Then he said angrily, "I bet I'll find at least one ore!"

But he didn't. Neither did anyone else. None of us has ever found even an ore since Bill found the krona.

Bill kept giving us candy while we walked toward home. Then he got the idea of having a contest to see who could keep his candy in his mouth the longest without its melting. He probably thought of that so the candy would last longer. Anyway, we all tried it. We each took a candy and sucked it as slowly as we could. After a while we stood in a circle in the road and stuck out our tongues to compare our candies. There was almost nothing left of them. We were halfway to Noisy Village by then and were standing right in front of Mr. Kind's cottage. He stuck his head out of the kitchen window and said we could take Agda's shoes to her. We pulled in our tongues quickly, because we didn't want him to see us comparing. Britta won the contest, and Karl put Agda's shoes in his schoolbag.

Then Olaf suggested that we should have a contest to see who could hold his breath the longest. But we waited until we were out of sight of the shoemaker's cottage, because he would have thought that was silly, too—to stand in the middle of the road and hold your breath.

We held our breath a long, long time. I told Mommy afterward that it wasn't because we held our breath so long that we had come home so late, but I was sure it had helped a little. Karl said that he won, but then Olaf said, "No, you didn't! Bill was bluer in the face than you."

The shoemaker has a meadow that floods in the spring and makes a little lake. There's a huge rock in the meadow and in the spring it sticks up out of the water like an island. When we got as far as the meadow, we stopped and rested a little while.

"I'd like to go out to that rock," said Karl. We all said we would too. So Karl went and got a couple of fence poles that he put down as a bridge over to the rock. We crept over, one at a time. It was nice to sit out there on the rock in the sunshine.

"If we only had something to eat," said Anna.

The candy was all gone. Then Karl looked in his schoolbag. There were Agda's shoes and a cheese sandwich that he hadn't been able to eat at lunchtime.

We pretended that the rock was a ship drifting around in the ocean, and that we were sailors who were going to die of starvation any day unless we were saved. Karl divided his sandwich into six equal parts for us. Then he said, "Friends, this is the only thing that separates us from death. But you must be as brave as your captain."

He was the captain, of course. Then he said the worst thing was that we didn't have any water, so we had to die of thirst too. But Bill said, "As far as I can see there's plenty of water. This whole meadow is full of water!"

Karl said Bill was stupid. The water around our ship was salty, and he would shoot anyone who tried to drink it. If you drink salt water you go crazy, he said.

Then he lay down on the rock and pretended he was delirious from hunger and thirst, and Bill said, "He must have drunk some salt water himself."

Karl got down on his knees and folded his hands and shouted, "Help, help!" as loudly as he could. In next to no time we heard someone running down the road, and it was the shoemaker! He thought Karl was really crying for help, and he was ever so mad!

"If you could get out there by yourselves, you can just get back by yourselves too," he said. "Darned kids!"

But he walked out in the water anyway and lifted us down from the rock one at a time and put us up on dry land. Of course he was wearing rubber boots, and he fussed at us the whole time. But it was nice of him anyway to come and save us, although it was completely unnecessary. We didn't dare say that, of course.

We hurried away as fast as we could. He yelled after us that he was sick and tired of Noisy Village children, and next time we'd better leave his fence poles alone.

When we had gone quite a way I happened to look at Karl's schoolbag, and then I said, "What have you done with Agda's shoes?"

Karl looked foolish. He'd left the shoes lying on the rock! He had put them down when he was fishing the cheese sandwich out of his bag. All of us turned around because we thought it would be too bad to let him go back alone.

The shoes were there on the rock, all right, wrapped in newspaper. The shoemaker had taken away the fence poles, but, seeing it was so warm and sunny, Karl suggested that we should all take off our shoes and stockings and wade out. It wasn't really so terribly cold in the water. We pretended the rock was a wrecked ship and we were pirates who had to climb aboard to save a valuable treasure—Agda's shoes. We pretended that there were lots of other pirates who were guarding the treasure on the wreck. We ran around in the water and shot at those pirates. Karl led us, and we climbed up on the wreck with knives between our teeth. Well, they were only sticks, but we pretended they were knives. Finally we all got up on the rock. Karl swung Agda's shoes over his head and yelled, "The loot is ours! Death to anyone who approaches us now!"

At that very second the shoemaker came back! He was the only one who approached us now. Poor thing, I really felt sorry for him when he saw us, because then he understood that he had saved us in vain. He stood there a long while with his mouth wide open and didn't say a word. We sat there on the rock, as quietly as mice. Finally the shoemaker came to life.

"Get away from there!" he yelled. "You'd better get away before I get hold of you!"

We jumped down, splashed ashore, picked up our shoes and stockings, and ran as fast as we could. The shoemaker yelled after us that it was certainly strange that we couldn't stay in Noisy Village to make nuisances of ourselves there.

We walked home and didn't stop any more—except to look at a bird's nest Bill knew about in a tree. We climbed up, one at a time, and saw four little light blue eggs in it. Bill has eggs like that in his collection, but he is very careful about birds and birds' nests, so we looked very quietly.

This didn't take very long, but when I told Mommy about it she said, "Now I'm beginning to understand why you can't possibly get home from school before five in the afternoon."

Karl told Agda that she would get her shoes the next day. He had them in a very safe place, he said, and she didn't need to worry that they would get lost during the night. They were guarded by pirates and a very angry shoemaker.

9 ANNA AND I
MAKE PEOPLE HAPPY

ONE DAY at school Miss Johnson said we should always try to make other people happy. We should never do anything that would make anyone feel bad, she said. Well, that same afternoon Anna and I sat on our back stairs talking, and we decided to start making people happy right away.

The trouble was that we didn't quite know how to go about it. We decided to start with Agda, so we went into the kitchen, where she was scrubbing the floor.

"Don't step on the floor when it's wet," she said.

"Agda," I said, "can you tell me something that we could do to make you happy?"

"Yes, if you would get out of the kitchen while I'm scrubbing the floor, I would be very happy," said Agda.

We went outside again. It wasn't much fun to make people happy that way. Anyway, I don't think that's what Miss Johnson meant.

Mommy was in the orchard, picking apples. I walked

over and said, "Mommy, tell me something I can do to make you happy."

"I'm already happy," Mommy said.

That was too bad, but I didn't want to give up, so I said, "But couldn't I do something to make you even happier?"

"You don't have to do anything except keep right on being my good little girl," said Mommy. "Then I'll be quite happy enough."

So I went back to Anna, and I said that Miss Johnson probably had no idea how hard it was to find someone to make happy.

"I know, let's try Grandfather," Anna said.

So we went to Grandfather's.

"Are my little friends coming to see me?" said Grandfather. "That makes me very happy!"

Wasn't that a shame! We had hardly come inside the door, and Grandfather was already happy. There was nothing left for us to do.

"No, Grandfather," said Anna. "Don't tell us that you're *already* happy. We want to do something to *make* you happy. You have to help us think of something, because Miss Johnson says we have to make other people happy."

"You could perhaps read the paper to me. That would make me happy," said Grandfather.

"Well, yes, but we do that so often that there's nothing special about it."

All of a sudden Anna said, "Grandfather, you hardly

ever get to leave this room. Wouldn't you be awfully happy if we took you for a walk?"

Grandfather didn't look very happy at the suggestion, but he promised to go with us. Anna and I walked on either side of Grandfather and led him, because he can't see where he's going. We took him all around Noisy Village and talked and told him things the whole time. The wind had started to blow, and it rained a little, but we didn't mind because we were bound and determined to make Grandfather happy.

As we were walking along Grandfather said, "Don't you

think we've walked enough now? I'd like to go to bed."

We led Grandfather back to his room. He undressed right away and crept into his bed, although it wasn't night yet. Anna tucked him in. He looked a little tired.

Before we left, Anna said, "Grandfather, what's the nicest thing that's happened to you all day?"

We both thought that he'd say that the walk had been the nicest thing. But Grandfather said, "The nicest thing that's happened to me today—well, snuggling down in my nice warm bed. I feel very tired."

Afterward Anna and I had to do our homework, so we didn't have time to make any more people happy that day. The next day we still weren't quite sure that we knew the right way to make people happy, so we decided to ask Miss Johnson about it. Miss Johnson said that often very little was needed. You could perhaps sing a song for someone who was sick and alone, or give a flower to someone who never got flowers, or speak kindly to someone who felt bashful and out of place.

Anna and I decided to try again. That afternoon I heard Agda tell Mommy that Karen was sick. She lives by herself in a little house at the edge of the woods. I ran over to Anna right away and said, "What luck! Karen is sick. Come on, let's go over there and sing to her!"

Karen seemed quite pleased to see us, but she probably wondered why we didn't bring her anything in a basket, because we usually do.

"Do you want us to sing something for you?" I asked.

"Sing?" said Karen, and looked surprised. "Why?"

"To make you happy," said Anna.

"All right, go ahead," said Karen.

We started with "Oh, Susannah," and then we sang "The Farmer in the Dell," all seven verses. Karen didn't look any happier than she had when we started. So then we sang "Little Miss Muffet," and "The Old Woman Who Lived in a Shoe," and "Mary Had a Little Lamb," and a couple more songs, but Karen still didn't look a bit happier.

We were beginning to get hoarse but we weren't going to stop until we had made her very happy. We were just starting "Little Bo-Peep" when Karen climbed out of bed and said, "You can stay and sing as much as you like, but I'm going to take a little walk."

Anna and I didn't think it was worth trying any longer, so we said good-by to Karen.

"Perhaps it would work better to give flowers to someone who never gets flowers," said Anna.

We were just wondering whom we could find to give flowers to when we saw Oscar, the hired man, walking into the barn. We ran after him, and I said, "Oscar, have you ever had any flowers given to you?"

"I should say not. I'm not dead yet, am I?" said Oscar.

Poor thing, he probably thought you only had flowers

at your funeral. Anna looked at me, pleased because we had found someone who never got flowers. We ran right over to the North Farm pasture and picked a bouquet of heather and brought it down to the barn. Oscar was pushing a wheelbarrow full of manure which he was going to throw on the compost heap behind the barn.

"Here are some flowers for you, Oscar," we said and handed him the bouquet.

Oscar thought at first that we were joking with him, and wouldn't take the bouquet until we said he *had* to take it. A little while later Anna and I were hunting for a rabbit that had got out of its cage, and we walked by the compost heap. There lay Oscar's bouquet!

"I'm beginning to think Miss Johnson is wrong," said Anna. So we decided to stop making people happy.

But a little later that afternoon Anna and I came into our kitchen and found a man sitting there. He was Mr. Swenson from Stubby Point, and he looked very out of place. He had come to buy a pig from us, and my brothers had gone to get Daddy, who was plowing the big field. Mr. Swenson sat waiting in our kitchen.

Anna looked at him and then pulled me into a corner and whispered, "Don't you think he looks bashful and out of place? Why don't we try just once more. Let's speak kindly to him, the way Miss Johnson said."

So that's what we decided to do. Usually Anna and I can talk a blue streak, but now, when we wanted to speak kindly to Mr. Swenson to make him happy, we couldn't think of a thing to say.

I thought and thought, and finally I said, "It's a wonderful day, isn't it?"

Mr. Swenson didn't answer, so I tried once more.

"It's a beautiful day, isn't it?" I said.

"Uhuh," said Mr. Swenson.

Then it was quiet. After a while I said, "Yesterday was a beautiful day also."

"Uhuh," said Mr. Swenson.

I looked at Anna because I thought she could help me a little. Anna said, "Tomorrow will probably be a beautiful day too."

"Uhuh," said Mr. Swenson.

Just then Daddy came across the yard, and Mr. Swenson got up and left. But when he had just gone out of the door he poked his head back in, grinned, and said, "And what was the weather like day before yesterday?"

"Perhaps we made him a little bit happy, anyway," said Anna later.

"Perhaps," I said, "but I've had enough. I'm not going to make any more people happy."

But we did, all the same, because the next day Miss Johnson told us that Martha, a girl in our class, wasn't coming back to school for a long time. She was very, very sick and had to stay in bed several months. That night, before I went to sleep, I lay awake thinking about Martha, and then I decided to give her Bella, my most beautiful doll. This was because I knew that Martha didn't have any toys at all.

In the morning when I told Anna that I was going to give Martha my doll, she went to get her nicest story book. And after school we went over to Martha's house. She was in bed and looked very pale. Never have I seen anyone as happy as Martha was when we put Bella and the story book beside her pillow and told her that she could keep them both. My, oh, my, how happy she was! She

hugged Bella and the story book and laughed and laughed. Then she called her mother to come and see her presents.

When we were outside the door, I said to Anna, "Isn't it funny, now we've made someone happy without even trying."

Anna looked surprised and said, "You're right! We have!" And then she said, "It was a lucky thing that we didn't start singing for Martha, because I think it makes people happier to get dolls and books."

"Children, anyway," I said.

10   THE BIG SNOWSTORM

Now i'm going to tell you about the big snowstorm that came just before Christmas. Daddy said it was the worst snowstorm he had ever seen.

Every day, from the very beginning of December, Karl had been saying, "I bet we won't have any snow for Christmas."

I felt sad every time he said it, because I wanted very

much to have snow. But one day after another went by, and still not the tiniest little flake fell. Then one day in the middle of the week before Christmas, while we were in school doing arithmetic, Bill suddenly said, "Look, it's snowing."

And it was. We were so happy that we all cheered, and Miss Johnson said that we should all stand up and sing "Now It Is Winter."

When we went out for recess the school yard was covered with a thin white layer. With our feet we made a track in the snow shaped like a figure eight. We ran around the eight all during recess.

Still Karl said, "I bet we won't have any more snow than this."

When we walked to school the next day, however, there was so much snow that we had to wade through it, and it was still snowing. But Karl said, "There won't be any more snow than this, and it'll probably melt before Christmas."

But that's where he was wrong. No sooner were we inside the school than it started snowing harder than ever. The air outside the window was perfectly white, and you couldn't even see across the yard. It kept on snowing all morning. And then the wind began to blow too. It stormed and snowed and snowed and stormed, and finally Miss Johnson got worried and said, "I don't know how you children from Noisy Village are going to get home today."

She wondered if we would like to spend the night with her, and of course we wanted to very much, but we knew that our fathers and mothers would get awfully worried if we didn't come home. So we said we couldn't stay, and Miss Johnson told us we better leave right away before it got dark.

At one o'clock we left school. My, how big the drifts were! And how the wind blew! We had to bend almost double when we walked.

"Well, Karl, is this enough snow for you?" asked Britta.

"It's not Christmas yet," said Karl, but we could hardly hear what he said because of the wind.

We walked and walked and walked. And we held hands so we wouldn't get lost. The snow reached way above my knees, and when it's that deep you don't get ahead very fast, I can tell you. The wind blew right through us so that our toes and fingers and noses got numb. Finally my legs were so tired that I told Karl I wanted to rest a little.

"Nothing doing," said Karl. Anna was tired too and wanted to rest, but Karl said it was too dangerous. Then Anna and I started to cry because we thought we would never get home again. We were only halfway then. But all of a sudden Olaf said, "Let's go to the shoemaker's. All he can do is chop our heads off."

Anna and I wanted to go to the shoemaker's even if he did chop our heads off.

The wind was so strong that we almost blew right

through the shoemaker's door. He didn't look very glad to see us.

"What are you children doing out in this kind of weather?" he said.

We didn't dare say that the weather had not been that bad when we had left home. We took off our coats and sat down to watch him while he mended shoes. We were hungry, but we didn't dare say so. The shoemaker made coffee for himself and ate sandwiches, but he didn't offer us any.

At dusk it stopped snowing and the wind stopped blowing, but the drifts were so high that we couldn't think how we were going to get home anyway. Oh, how I wanted to get home to Noisy Village and to Mommy and to my bed!

Suddenly we heard sleigh bells jingling out in the snow, so we ran to the window and looked. It was Daddy, driving the snow plow. We opened the door and called to him, and the shoemaker said, "Don't let the cold air in!"

Daddy was very happy when he saw us. He said he was only going to plow the road down to the big village, and then he'd pick us up on his way back.

That's what he did. Anna and I rode home on the snow plow, and the others walked behind. Now the road was smooth, so it was easy.

Mommy was standing at the kitchen window, looking worried, when we got home. Karl and Bill and I had hot beef broth with dumplings for supper, and it was the best food I'd ever tasted. I ate three platefuls. Afterward I went right to bed. It was wonderful. Mommy said she had had a feeling that Daddy should go out with the snow plow, because she was sure we'd be somewhere along the road. Wasn't it lucky that she'd had that feeling? Otherwise we would probably have had to stay at the shoemaker's all night.

11   SOON IT'LL BE CHRISTMAS

THE NEXT day the sun shone and the trees were all white with snow. Miss Johnson said she hadn't slept a wink all night. She had lain awake, wondering how we had managed in the snow.

Since it was the last day of school before Christmas, Miss Johnson read us a Christmas story. Everything felt wonderful that day, but just before we were going to leave came the best thing of all. Miss Johnson had written to Stockholm and ordered story books for all of us. A few weeks before, she had shown us a large sheet of paper with many pretty pictures of the covers of different books, so we could choose which ones we wanted to buy. I had ordered two, and Karl and Bill also had ordered two each. Mine had pictures of princes and princesses on the covers. Now, on the very last day of school before Christmas, Miss Johnson had received the books. She walked around and gave them out to us. I could hardly wait to get mine, but Mommy had said that we were not to read them until Christmas Eve.

Before we left school that day, we sang all the Christmas songs we knew, and Miss Johnson said she hoped we would have a Merry Christmas. I was sure that I would.

Britta and Anna and I ran to the store and bought red, yellow, green, white, and blue shiny paper, because we were going to make baskets to hang on the Christmas tree. Then we walked home. It was light and pretty outside.

As we were walking along, Britta took her book out of her schoolbag and smelled it. She let all of us smell it. New books smell so good that you can tell how much fun it's going to be to read them. Then Britta started to read. Her mother, too, had said that she should save her books until Christmas Eve, but Britta said she was only going to read a tiny little bit. After she had read the tiny little bit we all thought it was so terribly exciting that we begged her to read just a tiny little bit more. So she read a little bit more. But that didn't help, because when she had finished that part it was still just as exciting and we wanted to know what would happen next.

"I have to know if the prince got bewitched or not," said Karl.

So Britta read a little bit more. That's the way we kept on, and by the time we got home to Noisy Village she had read the whole book. Britta said that it didn't matter because she was going to read it over again on Christmas Eve anyway.

When we got to our house Mommy and Agda were

making the Christmas sausage, and the kitchen was a mess. As soon as we had eaten supper we went out and made a big snow lantern in our yard. Britta and Anna and Olaf came over and helped us. When we finished the lantern we put a candle inside.

In the linden tree there were lots of sparrows and bull-finches, and they looked so hungry that I ran and asked Daddy if we could put up the Christmas sheaves a little early. Daddy said we could, so we all ran down to the loft and got five oat sheaves that had been saved out for Christmas when they were threshing. We put them in the apple trees in our orchard, and it wasn't long before the birds were sitting in the trees eating the oats. They probably thought it was already Christmas Eve. The Christmas sheaves and the snow and everything were awfully pretty.

In the evening Britta and Anna and I sat in Grand-father's room and made Christmas-tree baskets. The boys were there too. First they said they weren't going to make any Christmas-tree baskets, but after a while they couldn't keep from doing it. We all sat around Grandfather's table to work. We made fifty-four baskets, which we divided evenly so that there were eighteen baskets for North Farm and eighteen for Middle Farm and eighteen for South Farm. Grandfather treated us to apples and barley-sugar when we finished. The whole time we sat there I kept thinking that the next day we were going to bake the ginger snaps. It was almost as much fun as Christmas Eve.

Right in the middle of it all Karl ran out to the yard and lighted the candle that we had put in the snow lantern. My, how pretty it looked in the dark! When I saw it shining so brightly out there, I couldn't help thinking about the Christmas song: "Christmas stands before the door, gives

a knock and smiles." I could almost see Christmas standing there, smiling, just like the snow lantern.

"I feel so sorry for you, Grandfather, because you can't
see the snow lantern," said Anna. "Do you want us to sing
for you instead?" Grandfather loves it when we sing. So
we sang the very song I had been thinking about: "Christmas Stands before the Door."

"Don't you think Christmas is fun?" Anna whispered to
me afterward. I said I did. It's more fun than anything
else I know.

12   CHRISTMAS IN NOISY VILLAGE

I DON'T know when Christmas starts in other places, but in Noisy Village it starts the day we bake ginger snaps. We have almost as much fun that day as on Christmas Eve. Karl and Bill and I each get a big chunk of ginger-snap dough, and we can bake it in the shape of anything we want. The last time we were to bake ginger snaps, Karl forgot all about it and went to the forest with Daddy to get wood. Right in the middle of the forest he remembered what day it was and rushed home so fast that the snow whirled around him, Daddy said.

Bill and I had already started to bake. It was just as well that Karl came a little late because the best ginger-snap mold we have is a pig, and when Karl is there it's almost impossible for Bill and me to get it. But this time we had baked ten pigs each before Karl came puffing home from the forest. How he hurried to catch up with us!

When we had almost finished baking we put all our last little pieces of dough together and made a big prize

cooky. We always do this. Then in the afternoon, when
all the ginger snaps had come out of the oven, we put 332

dried peas in a bottle and went around all over Noisy Village to let everyone guess how many peas there were. The one who made the closest guess would get the big cooky for a prize.

Karl carried the bottle, Bill carried the prize cooky, and I carried a notebook where I wrote down everyone's guess. Grandfather was the one who won the prize, and I was so glad. He guessed that there were 320 peas in the bottle, which was very close. Anna guessed that there were three *thousand* peas. Wasn't that crazy?

The day after we baked the ginger snaps was fun too, for then we went to the forest to cut the Christmas trees. All the fathers go along when we cut the Christmas trees— and all the children too, of course. The mothers have to stay at home and cook, poor things! We took our big sleigh, which we use for carrying the milk from Noisy Village to the dairy in the big village. Karl and Bill and I and Britta and Anna and Olaf rode in the sleigh. My daddy walked beside it and drove the horse. Olaf's and Britta's and Anna's daddies walked behind it and laughed and talked. All of us in the sleigh laughed and talked too.

There was so much snow in the forest that we had to shake it out of the fir trees to see if they were pretty or not. We cut three big fir trees, one for each farm. And then we cut a tiny little tree for Grandfather to have in his room, and another little one to give to Karen, because she lives all alone in her red cottage in the woods.

The night before Christmas Eve I felt sad because I didn't think Mommy and Agda could ever get everything ready for Christmas. It looked so messy all over the house, and especially in the kitchen. I cried a little after I had gone to bed.

Christmas Eve morning I woke up early and ran down to the kitchen in my nightie to see if it was still messy. But oh, my! how beautiful it was! There were new rag carpets on the floor; there was red and green and white curled tissue paper around the iron pole by the stove; there was a Christmas cloth on the big folding table; and all the copper kettles were polished. I was so happy that I gave Mommy a big hug. Karl and Bill came rushing in right after me, and Karl said that even his stomach felt Christmassy when he saw the rag carpets.

On Christmas Eve morning all of us Noisy Village children always go over to Karen's with a basket full of goodies from our mothers. But first we go to Grandfather to wish him a Merry Christmas and watch Britta and Anna decorate his little tree. We help a little too, although Britta and Anna prefer to do it by themselves. Of course Grandfather can't see what we hang on the tree, but when we tell him about it he says that he can see it inside his head.

When we walked over to Karen's cottage the weather was very beautiful, just the way it should be on Christmas Eve. The road that goes to Karen's cottage is so narrow that we could hardly see it under all the snow. Karl carried the basket, and Bill and Olaf the little fir tree. The boys wouldn't let Britta and Anna and me carry anything. My, how surprised Karen was when we came! Well, she probably was just pretending to be surprised, because she knows that we come every year. Karl unpacked everything in the basket and put it on the table, and Karen just shook her head and said, "My, my, it's too much, it's much too much!"

I didn't think that it was too much, but it was a lot: A large piece of ham, a sausage, a round cheese, coffee, ginger snaps, candles, candy, and I don't remember what all. We put the candles on Karen's tree and danced around it a little while to practice for later on that night. Karen was very happy, and she stood in the doorway and waved to us as we left.

When we got home Karl and Bill and I decorated our tree. Daddy helped us. We got the red apples that we were going to use on the tree out of the attic, and then we hung some of our ginger snaps on it. We put raisins and nuts in the baskets we had made in Grandfather's room. We also hung up the cotton angels that Mommy had used on her tree when she was little—and then, of course, a lot of flags and candles and candy. My, how pretty the tree was when it was finished!

Then it was time to "dip in the pot." Mommy gave us large slices of rye bread that Agda had baked, and we dipped them in the broth that the ham had cooked in. My,

how good it was! Then there was nothing to do but WAIT.
Karl said that times like those hours in the afternoon of
Christmas Eve, when you don't do anything but wait and
wait, are the kind of things people get gray hairs from.
We waited and waited and waited, and from time to time

I went to the mirror to see if I had any gray hairs yet. But strangely enough, my hair was just as yellow as ever. Bill hit the clock now and then, because he thought that it had stopped.

When it got dark, it was time at last to take our presents over to North Farm and South Farm. You can't do that when it's light because it wouldn't be exciting at all. Karl and Bill and I put on our red Santa Claus caps and Karl took the Santa Claus mask that he was going to wear later in the evening. (It's Karl who is Santa Claus at our house nowadays. When I was little I thought that there was a real Santa Claus, but I don't think so any more.) Then we took our packages and sneaked out into the dark. The sky was full of stars. I looked toward the forest, standing so dark and still, and imagined that perhaps there was a real Santa Claus living there who soon would come, pulling a sled loaded with Christmas presents. I almost wished that it were true.

There was no light in the kitchen at North Farm. We pounded on the back door, and then we opened it and threw our Christmas packages inside. Britta and Anna came rushing out and said that we had to come in and taste their Christmas cookies and candy. So we did, and they gave us Christmas packages too. Britta and Anna put on their Santa Claus masks, and we all went over to South Farm to see Olaf. He was sitting in their kitchen, and he was just waiting too. Skip barked like everything when he saw five Santa Clauses coming. Then Olaf put on a mask too, and we all ran out and played Santa Claus in the dark.

At last it was really Christmas Eve, and we ate supper at the folding table in the kitchen. There were candles on the table and an awful lot of food, but I didn't eat much except ham. I did eat porridge, of course, in case I should get the almond. The one who gets the almond in the porridge will surely get married during the coming year. But I didn't get it. It had broken in two, and Oscar the hired man and Agda each got a piece. How Karl and Bill and I laughed. Agda got cross and said the whole thing was probably one of our tricks. But how could we help it that the almond had broken in two?

We made up rhymes to the porridge too. Karl made up this one:

> You saw the almond break in two,
> So Oscar will marry you, guess who.

We thought that was pretty good, but Agda didn't think so. She got a little more cheerful afterward, when we all helped her to dry the dishes. We did that so we could get ready sooner and start giving out the presents.

When we finished we went into the dining room. The tree was lighted and so were the candles on the table. I got goose flesh the way I always do when anything's very beautiful and exciting. Daddy read to us from the Bible about the Christ Child. I read some terribly pretty verses that start this way: "Oh, little Lord Jesus, asleep in the hay." It goes on to say in those verses that the Christ Child should really have a whole lot of Christmas presents and a cake. That's what I think too. But instead we're the ones who get all the presents.

While the rest of us sang "Silent Night," Karl slipped out and in a little while he came back, dressed as Santa Claus, with a big sack on his back.

"Are there any good children here?" he asked.

"Yes, there are good children here," said Bill. "But we have a real brat too, whose name is Karl. He seems to be out at the moment, thank goodness."

"I've heard about him," said Santa Claus. "He's the nicest boy in this country. He should have more presents than anyone else."

But he didn't get any more than anyone else. We all got the same number of presents. I got a new doll, and three books, a game, a piece of cloth for a dress, mittens, and all kinds of other things. I got fifteen presents altogether.

I had made a tea cloth with cross stitching for Mommy. She was very happy when she got it. I had bought a calendar for Daddy. He was happy too. I like it when people are happy about the Christmas presents I give them. It's as much fun as getting presents yourself. I gave tin soldiers to Karl and Bill.

Afterward we danced around the tree, and everyone from North Farm and South Farm came and helped us.

Grandfather came too, although he couldn't dance. I think we danced to "Now It's Christmas Again" and "Cut, Cut the Oats" at least twenty times.

That night I put all my Christmas presents on the table by my bed, so that I'd be able to see them first thing when I woke up in the morning.

Christmas is wonderful! It's really too bad that it isn't Christmas a little more often.

13   AUNT JENNY'S PARTY

THE MOST fun during our whole vacation was the party the Sunday after Christmas at Aunt Jenny's. She lives on a farm way on the other side of the big village.

Everybody in Noisy Village was invited, and we had to ride for hours to get there. There was a sleigh from each farm.

Mommy woke us up very early and bundled us up in an awful lot of sweaters and scarfs. I was sure I would suffocate before I got to the party, but then Mommy came with still another shawl to put over my head! I said that if I had to go to Aunt Jenny's looking like a freak, I wouldn't go at all.

We rode in our wicker sleigh with Daddy driving. Behind us came the South Farm sleigh, and the North Farm sleigh came last. All the bells sounded very gay. We were so happy that we began to sing, but Mommy said we had to stop because we'd get too much cold air in our lungs. So instead we shouted a lot of messages to Olaf, who was in the sleigh behind us, and he yelled them on to Britta and Anna.

"If she gives us herring salad, I'm going home," yelled Karl.

"So am I," yelled Olaf.

Then Olaf explained to Britta and Anna what they were talking about, and after a while Olaf yelled to us that Britta and Anna would also go home if they had to eat herring salad.

We did have herring salad, but we didn't go home, because there were ever so many other kinds of food and we didn't have to eat the herring salad.

Aunt Jenny has three girls of her own, and there were crowds of other children at the party. We played in a big room on the second floor all day long except when we ate. We really got tired of all that food, because as soon as we had started on a new game, Aunt Jenny would come and tell us that now we had to go down and eat some more. Grownups don't seem to do *anything* but eat when they're at a party.

Aunt Jenny's oldest girl's name is Nanna. We pretended that Nanna was a witch who lived in a closet next to the playroom. The closet was her cottage, and the playroom was a large forest. Just as we were walking through the forest, picking berries, out came the witch from her cottage and caught us. We were as scared as if she had been a real witch! There was a big box in the closet, and this was the witch's oven. She tried to cook Karl in it, but he got out just at the last minute, thank goodness.

"I do smell a little burned, though," said Karl.

Sometimes the witch rushed at us and cried, "Petrified!"
When she said this everyone had to stop perfectly still
in the middle of whatever he was doing and not move a
muscle. Once when the witch cried, "Petrified," Karl was

caught standing on one leg with his tongue stuck out, his fingers poked in his ears, and his eyes crossed.

He had to stand still, looking like that, until the witch came and broke the spell. How we laughed at him!

Aunt Jenny's girls had a beautiful dolls' house in the corner of the playroom. Anna and I couldn't help going over there to look at it every few minutes. There was a kitchen in the dolls' house and a dining room and a bed room and a living room. A very fine doll family lived there. Nanna said their names were Count and Countess Golden-mushroom. They had a pretty little girl who sat in a chair in the living room, whose name was Isabella Goldenmush-room.

When the grownups had finally finished eating, they came up and played with us too. First we played blind man's bluff. Then we played pawn games. I gave my little gold heart as a pawn. To get it back I was sentenced to turn three somersaults. I did, and then I got my gold heart. Olaf was sentenced to say the name of his beloved three times into the fireplace, and just think, he said "Lisa" three times. Karl started to laugh, and I was terribly embarrassed. But Olaf looked full of mischief and said to me, "I meant my mother, of course. Her name is Lisa too."

Daddy was sentenced to jump around the whole room like a frog. I had never seen Daddy jump like a frog before, and it was terribly funny! But the worst sentence was Aunt Jenny's. She was told to climb up on the table, stand on one leg, and crow like a rooster. She wouldn't do it, though.

"Nonsense," she said. "How could the table hold me, fat as I am?"

She was probably right. Aunt Jenny weighs almost two hundred pounds.

We played for a long time and had a lot of fun. But now and then Anna and I stole over to the dolls' house to say hello to Isabella Goldenmushroom.

The best thing about Aunt Jenny's party was that we were going to stay all night. I like to spend the night in strange houses, everything feels so different and wonderful. It also smells quite different from home. There were fourteen of us children at the party, and we were all going to sleep in a row on the floor in the playroom. Just think what fun it was to lie on the floor! We had straw mattresses but no sheets, just blankets. When we had gone to bed, all the grownups came up to look at us.

"Here lies Sweden's youth by the yard," said Daddy.

When the grownups had left, we were supposed to go to sleep. But I think it's almost impossible to get fourteen children to be quiet enough for anyone to be able to sleep. Nanna told us about a big treasure that some knight had buried near there long, long ago. Karl wanted to go out and dig for it in the middle of the night. But Nanna said that nobody could find the treasure because it was bewitched. Then I must have gone to sleep because I don't remember hearing any more.

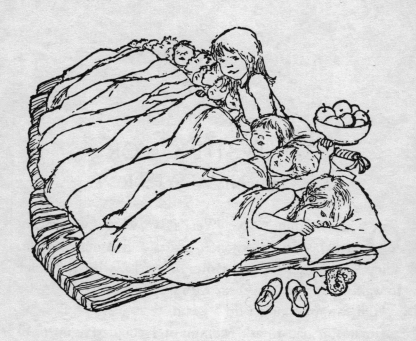

We didn't go home until late in the afternoon of the next day. It was quite dark before we got to our village. We didn't yell from one sleigh to another on the way home because we were so tired. I lay back and looked up at all the stars. There were so many of them, and they were so far away. Then I crept down under the fur rug and sang quietly to myself, so that Karl and Bill would not hear me:

> Twinkle, twinkle, little star,
> How I wonder what you are.

I hope that we can go to a Christmas party at Aunt Jenny's next year too.

14 WAITING FOR
THE NEW YEAR

O N THE morning of New Year's Eve, when I was having
breakfast in the kitchen, Britta and Anna came in.
They looked excited, and Britta said, "Lisa, do you want
to wait up for the New Year with us?"

"Oh, yes, of course I do," I said.

But first I had to ask Mommy if I could stay up until
midnight, when the New Year comes in. She said I could,
so we decided right away that we would wait up for it in
my room. Mommy said that she would give us apples and
nuts and root beer so we could have a real feast.

A few minutes later Karl and Bill came in, and I said,
"Britta and Anna and I are going to wait up and watch for
the New Year tonight!"

Karl said, "So are we. We decided that a long time ago."

But I'm sure he decided to wait up for the New Year
just because we were going to.

We ran over and asked Grandfather if he wanted to wait
up with us, but he said that he always got too sleepy at

night. Grandfather is so very, very nice! He went into his closet and got several little pieces of lead which he gave us.

"You can't have a real New Year's wake without melting lead," he said.

He told us that you can find out what's going to happen to you during the coming year if you melt lead and pour it into cold water. If the lead takes the shape of a coin, for instance, it means that you'll get a lot of money.

Grandfather let us borrow a little ladle the boys use when they cast lead soldiers.

We didn't tell the boys that Grandfather had given us the lead.

We had fun that evening! My room was all fixed up. I had taken out the rag carpets and beaten them, and had dusted everywhere. I had a pretty candlestick with five candles that I put in the center of the table, with the bowl of apples and the jug of root beer and the dish of nuts arranged around it. When Britta and Anna arrived, the candles were burning beautifully. I had a fire burning in the fireplace too.

"I like New Year's wakes!" said Anna.

The boys were waiting for the New Year in Karl's and Bill's room. A big dark attic separates their room from mine, and just as we had settled down to wait we heard footsteps there. A little while later we heard a terrible bang, but we didn't pay any attention to it. We knew that it was the boys who were trying to lure us out into the attic. We had heard Karl's cap pistol before.

After that nothing more happened, so we began to get curious and peeked out through a crack in our door. The attic was perfectly quiet and dark. Then we decided to sneak across and look through the boys' keyhole to see what they were doing.

"I don't see a thing," said Britta, who looked first. "They aren't even there."

"I wouldn't be surprised if they've gone to sleep and forgotten all about the New Year," said Anna.

"Well, they're certainly the ones to hold New Year's wakes," I said. "Let's get one of Karl's caps and wake them up."

Suddenly something went bang right behind us, and we were so startled that we nearly jumped out of our skins.

"Those villains are hiding in the attic," cried Anna.

I ran for my flashlight, and we flashed it in all the corners and behind all the old trunks and clothes, but found no boys.

"This is most peculiar," said Britta.

There was another loud bang right behind us. It was a firecracker this time.

"Just wait until I get hold of that Karl," said Britta fiercely. "I'll give him a beating he'll never forget."

"Yes, do that, by all means." Karl's voice came from high over our heads.

And up there on the beams under the ceiling sat Karl and Bill and Olaf. Were we ever furious.

"How's your old sissy-wake coming?" Karl asked.

"Very well, thank you," we said. "We are just going to start melting lead to see what's going to happen next year."

That made them curious, I can tell you. They followed us to my room, and when they saw how nice it looked with candles and a fire and everything, they decided to move over with us. Bill brought their apples and nuts and root beer.

Then we melted the lead in the ladle in the fireplace, and each one poured a little into the water in my washbasin. Karl poured first. When his chunk of lead had hardened, he fished it out and examined it carefully. Then he said, "It looks as if I were going to become a king, because this is a king's crown."

Anna laughed. "It looks more like a book to me! That means that you're going to have to go to school all of next year."

My chunk of lead was funny-looking. "I think it's a bicycle," said Olaf.

That made me happy, because I want a bicycle very, very much.

When we'd finished pouring lead we sat down on the floor in front of the fireplace and told stories. Britta tells *such* good stories. We ate lots of apples and nuts and drank root beer. And then we "nutted." Britta and Anna knew a wonderful way to do it. Britta held some nuts in her hand, but we didn't know how many.

First Britta said, "The stove is smoking!"

And then Anna answered, "I'll have to run up to the attic!"

And then Britta asked, "How many boys will you take along?"

"Five," said Anna. Britta had exactly five nuts in her

hand, she had to give them to Anna, and Anna had won the nutting. We nutted in lots of other ways too, but Anna was so clever that when we finished she had twice as many nuts as anyone else.

All at once Bill began to yawn. Finally he said that he was going to lie down on my bed to wait for the New Year. He did lie down, but it wasn't two minutes before he was fast asleep. Mommy and Daddy came to say good night to us, because they weren't going to stay up till midnight.

A little later we asked Karl what time it was.

"Half past ten," he said.

I think New Year's Eve is probably longer than other

nights. It seemed as if midnight would never come. But finally it did. We tried to wake up Bill to tell him the New Year had arrived, but that was absolutely impossible. We turned out the light and stood by the window, looking out into the darkness to see if the New Year was riding in. We couldn't see a thing. But anyway we drank root beer and cried, "Happy New Year!"

We decided that we would have a New Year's wake every year because it was so much fun.

I was beginning to feel that I wanted nothing on earth so much as to go to bed—but there was Bill, fast asleep. We all carried him by his arms and legs to his own bed. He didn't wake up at all. Karl undressed him and put on his pajamas and then tied one of my hair ribbons in his hair.

"We'll leave it there until tomorrow so Bill can see that he had a good time at the New Year's wake," said Karl.

15 THOSE MISCHIEVOUS BOYS

WHEN Christmas vacation was over, there was still so much snow that we could ride our push-sleighs to school. We have three push-sleighs. Sometimes we fastened all three together to make one long sleigh with several seats.

Miss Johnson said it was nice to see us again, and I thought it was nice to see her too because I like her so much. She treated all the children to candy because it was the first day of school. She'd bought the candy in Stockholm, where she spent her vacation. That's the only time I've ever eaten candy bought in Stockholm.

It was fun to see all the children from the big village again. During recess the girls traded bookmarks as usual. I traded with Anna-Greta, a girl in our class who has many, many bookmarks. I gave her a basket of flowers and a Santa Claus bookmark, and she gave me a princess. It was almost the prettiest bookmark I had ever seen, so I think I made a good bargain.

In the winter the boys usually throw snowballs at each other during recess. In the spring they shoot marbles, and the girls play hopscotch. When the boys have nothing else to do they fight, and during class they get into all kinds of mischief, whether it's winter or spring. Miss Johnson says she thinks there is something that makes boys' fingers itch so they can't help doing mischief. I think that Karl's fingers must itch all the time! One day he brought to school a

funny little pig that Bill had given him. It was made of rubber, and you could blow it up. When you let the air out, the pig squealed loudly.

Our class was reading—reading is my favorite subject— and it was my turn to read aloud. The story was about Gustaf Vasa.

"Then the king dissolved in tears," I said. And just as I spoke the words we heard a long, sad wail that sounded like Gustaf Vasa dissolving in tears. But it wasn't; it was Karl's pig. All the children laughed, and Miss Johnson looked as if she were going to laugh too, but she didn't. Karl had to stand in the corner for the rest of the lesson period. So did the pig.

But Karl isn't the only one who gets into mischief. All the boys are about the same. One day Miss Johnson had to go to a teachers' meeting, and we were supposed to go on with drawing and arithmetic by ourselves. Miss Johnson told Britta to sit at her desk and take charge.

But Miss Johnson hadn't more than stepped outside the door when the boys started to act up.

"Miss Britta, Miss Britta," they called and waved their hands.

"What do you want?" said Britta.

"We want to go out," they all yelled.

And Bill said, "Have you heard, Miss Britta, that the potatoes are growing well this year?"

Britta said, "Yes, I think I have heard that."

And Bill said, "Then you must have very good ears, Miss Britta."

Karl raised his hand and asked if he couldn't show Miss Britta what he had been drawing. He took his drawing pad to Britta, and the whole page was covered with black crayon.

"What is this supposed to be?" asked Britta.

"It's supposed to be five black cats in a dark closet," said Karl.

Britta didn't think that it was any fun at all to be a teacher and she was glad when our real teacher came back. Miss Johnson asked if the children had been good. Britta said, "Not the boys."

So Miss Johnson scolded the boys and said they would all have to stay after school a whole hour and do arithmetic. And do you know, during recess a boy named Steve went over to Britta and said, "Tattletale, tattletale!" and hit her over the head with his schoolbag. Wasn't that mean!

When we were walking home Britta told Anna and me that she never wanted to be a teacher again in her whole life.

We walked as slowly as we could so that Karl and Bill and Olaf could catch up with us. We knew that if they got home a whole hour later than we did our mothers would probably wonder what happened, and the boys would be punished again.

16   EASTER IN NOISY VILLAGE

Now I'm going to tell you about last Easter in Noisy Village.

On Easter Eve, Mommy and Daddy were going to a party at the minister's in the big village, so they let Karl and Bill and me have an egg party at our house. Mommy owns the Noisy Village chicken farm, as I said before, and so we have a great many eggs. Bill thinks his Albertina lays almost all the eggs.

We ate supper in the kitchen. The table looked beautiful, with a blue cloth and our yellow Easter plates. There were birch branches in a vase, and Karl and Bill and I had painted all the eggs red and yellow and green. Eggs should be those colors all the time, I think, because they look so nice. We had written verses on the eggs.

Bill's hen

poems

> Anna, you must eat this in a flash,
> Or you might get corned-beef hash,

it said on one of the eggs. Karl had written that verse, but Bill didn't think it was very good.

"Who ever thought of giving anyone corned-beef hash for Easter?" he said.

"How do you know what people might have thought of giving for Easter?" said Karl.

> "This is an egg for Ann,
> Instead of a frying pan,

Do you think that is better?" he asked.

Bill didn't think so. Anyway, we didn't have time to change the verse because just then Britta and Anna and Olaf arrived. At supper we had a race to see who could eat the most eggs. I could only eat three, but Olaf ate six.

"Albertina is a good hen," Bill said when we had finished. Afterward we were going to hunt for the Easter eggs filled with candy which Mommy had hidden. Every Easter Karl and Bill and I each get a large egg filled with lots and lots of candy. But this year Mommy said that if we would be satisfied with eggs that were a little smaller, she would buy some for Britta and Anna and Olaf too. Then we could give them as a surprise at our party. Of course we wanted to do this. It was hard to find the eggs, Mommy had hidden them so cleverly. Mine was in the cupboard where we keep the pots and pans. It was made of silver with little flowers.

Inside there was a little chicken made of almond paste, and lots of candy.

We were allowed to stay up as long as we wanted to, since it was Easter Eve. Agda was out with Oscar, and we were alone in the house, so we turned out all the lights and played hide-and-seek in the dark. We counted "Eeny, meeny, miney, mo," and Bill was the first one to be blind-folded. I found a good hiding place in the dining-room window behind the curtain. Bill tiptoed right by me several times, but he didn't find me.

But Britta was the one who found the best hiding place of all. Daddy's rubber boots stood out in the hall, and above them hung the big coat that he wears when he drives to the dairy with the milk. Well, Britta climbed down in the boots and wrapped the coat around her. When we couldn't find her, we turned on the lights and all of us hunted for her, but we still couldn't find her. Then we called, "You're free to come out!" But she just stood there, quiet as a mouse. Daddy's boots and coat looked just as usual, so how could we dream that Britta was inside them?

"Perhaps she is dead and gone forever," said Olaf.

Then we heard a giggle from inside the coat, and Britta stepped out, wearing Daddy's big boots. She wanted to play Puss in Boots, but Anna said it was time to go over to Grandfather's and make eggnog. So we did.

We took eggs and sugar and glasses to Grandfather's room. Grandfather was sitting in his rocking chair in front of the fire, and he was very glad when we came. We sat down on the floor in front of the fire and whipped eggnog very hard so that it splashed around us. Anna whipped Grandfather's for him because he couldn't see to do it him-self. I told him about my Easter egg made of silver with little flowers.

Then Grandfather told us about the olden days when children didn't have any Easter eggs filled with candy. Do you know that one Easter, when Grandfather was a little boy, it was so cold that his daddy had to use an ax to break the ice on the barrel of water that stood in the kitchen? And there were no Easter eggs to cheer him up! Poor little Grandfather!

17   THE LAST DAY OF SCHOOL

IT'S fun when summer comes. Everything is fun from the very day we finish school. This year the fun really started the afternoon before the last day. Then we decorated the schoolroom with flowers and branches. All the Noisy Village children had cut birch branches and picked primroses and almond flowers. You can't have a special school for only six children, so we have to walk a long way to school in the big village. The flowers were a little wilted when we arrived, but when we put them in water they freshened up again. We hung Swedish flags by the blackboard and put strings of birch leaves and lots of flowers all around the room. The whole school looked and smelled lovely.

When we had finished decorating we practiced the songs that we were going to sing at the closing exercises the next morning. The weather was beautiful and it took us a long time to get home because we played a game on the way. Karl said that we could walk only on the stones at the edge of the road. We pretended that if we stepped on the ground we would drop dead. All of a sudden Olaf stepped on the ground and Bill said, "Now you are dead."

"I am not," said Olaf. "Look how alive I am"—and he wriggled and kicked about. We all laughed.

Then we walked on the fence. Karl said, "Who do you think decided that people always had to walk on the road?"

Britta said that it was probably some grownup.

"Probably," said Karl.

We walked on top of the fence a long time and had such fun that I thought that I would never want to walk on the road again. An old man came by on a milk wagon and said, "Look at those crows walking on top of the fence."

But the next day, when we were going to the closing exercises, we couldn't walk on the fence because we were all so dressed up. I had on a brand new dress with red polka dots, and Britta and Anna had on blue dresses with ruffles. And we all had on hair ribbons and new shoes.

All the parents sat in the schoolroom and listened to us answer the questions at the exam. I answered all mine right but Bill didn't. He said that seven times seven was fifty-six. Karl turned around and looked at him, so Bill said, "No, I mean forty-six."

This was wrong too. It's really forty-nine. I know that because I have heard the other children say it. I have already learned it, although my class hasn't started multiplication tables yet. There are only twenty-three children in

the whole school, so we all sit in the same room and learn things like that from one another.

When we had finished the program and sung all the songs we had practiced, Miss Johnson said, "Good-by, all of you. And have a good time this summer."

When she said that, I felt my heart beating a bit faster.

All the Noisy Village children had got good grades. We compared them on the way home. Bill's weren't quite as good as the rest, but anyway he passed.

That evening we played ball down on the road. All of a sudden the ball flew over and fell among the currant bushes, so I ran to look for it. And guess what I found there! All the way back under a currant bush were eleven eggs. I was very happy, because one of our hens had laid them. She is stubborn and won't lay her eggs in the henhouse but lays them all outdoors. Karl and Bill and I had been trying to find them for a long time, but she is very smart and won't let us see where she goes. Mother had said that she would give us five ore for every egg we found. Now I found enough eggs for fifty-five ore, but I hadn't found the ball.

"Let's use the eggs for balls," said Karl. "Then there'll be scrambled eggs all over Noisy Village."

But I put the eggs in my apron and took them to Mother and got my fifty-five ore. I counted out five ore to give to each of the other children and put the rest in my money bank that I can lock with a little key. The key hangs on a nail way in the back of my closet.

When I got back Anna had found the ball and we played with it for several hours. We went to bed that night much later than usual, but it didn't matter, because it was summer vacation and we could sleep as long as we wanted to the next day.

18   ANNA AND I GO SHOPPING

THE store where we buy sugar and coffee and things like that, is in the big village, close to the school. When Mommy needs some groceries she usually asks me to get them for her after school. But during the summer vacation we have to make a special trip. One day Mommy said, "Lisa, there's nothing else to do. You'll just have to run down to the store for me."

It was a beautiful day, and I thought it would be fun to go shopping, so I said, "Sure, I'd love to. What do you want?"

Mommy said we'd probably better write a list. But we couldn't find a pencil, so I said, "Never mind. I can remember it all."

Then Mommy told me all the things I should buy: six ounces of yeast and a piece of Bologna sausage of the best quality, a package of ginger, some sewing needles, a can of anchovies, a bag of almonds, and a bottle of vinegar.

"I'm sure I'll remember it all," I said.

Just then Anna came rushing into our kitchen and asked me if I'd go to the store with her.

"Sure," I said. "I was just going to ask you to come with me."

Anna was wearing her new red cap and carried a basket on her arm. I put on my new green cap and took a basket on my arm too.

Anna was going to buy soap, a pound of coffee, two pounds of sugar, and two yards of elastic tape. Also she was to get a piece of Bologna sausage of the best quality, just as I was. Anna hadn't written down what she was going to buy either.

Before we left we went up to Grandfather's room to ask if there was anything he needed from the store, and he asked us to buy him some barley-sugar and a bottle of camphor liniment.

Just as we were leaving through the gate, Olaf's mother came running out onto their porch.

"Are you going to the store?" she called.

"Yes," we said.

"Oh, please would you buy a few things for me?" she asked.

We said we'd love to. She wanted us to buy a spool of white thread, number 40 and a bottle of vanilla.

"And wait, what else was it I wanted?" she said, looking thoughtful.

"A piece of Bologna sausage of the best quality?" I suggested.

"Yes, that was it," said Olaf's mother. "How could you guess?"

Then Anna and I left, and we were a little worried for fear we wouldn't be able to remember everything. First we recited all the things to each other out loud, but we soon got tired of that. We walked along arm in arm, swinging our baskets back and forth. The sun was shining and the trees smelled good. Then we made up songs about what we were to get. We sang, as loudly as we could, "A piece of Bologna sausage of the best quality." It sounded quite pretty. This is the way we did it. First I sang, "A piece of Bologna sausage," in a slow, romantic melody, and then Anna struck up, "Of the best quality, of the best quality," in a fast, happy tune. Sometimes we sang the words in a melody that was good to march to. But finally we settled for one that was sad all the way through and very beautiful. It was so beautiful that we almost began to cry.

"My, how sad it is about Bologna sausage," Anna said when we finally reached the store.

There were a lot of people in the store so we had to wait a long time, really much longer than we should have, because grownups seem to think that it doesn't matter how long children have to wait. They always push ahead. But finally Uncle Emil himself came out into the store. We know him. He started to ask how everyone in Noisy Village was, and if we had eaten lots of eggs during Easter, and if we weren't going to get married soon.

"We certainly are *not*," we said.

"And what do the ladies wish to buy today?" asked Uncle Emil. He always talks silly like that, but I like him anyway. He has a pencil behind his ear and a little red mustache. He always treats us to sourballs that he keeps in a big jar.

First Anna told him everything that she was supposed to buy for her mother and for Grandfather. Uncle Emil weighed everything and wrapped it in packages while Anna talked.

Then it was my turn to tell him everything I was going to get for Mommy and Olaf's mother. Both Anna and I thought as hard as we could so that we wouldn't forget anything. Uncle Emil gave us two sourballs apiece, and we left.

When we had walked as far as the fork in the road where we turn to Noisy Village, I said, "Anna do you remember if I bought yeast?"

Anna couldn't at all remember. We started squeezing all the packages in my basket. There was nothing that felt like yeast. So we had to go back to the store. Uncle Emil laughed at us and gave us the yeast and some more sourballs. Then we left.

Just as we came to the fork in the road again, Anna cried, "Grandfather's camphor liniment!"

"I've never seen the like!" I said.

There was nothing else we could so but go back to the store. How Uncle Emil laughed at us! He gave us the camphor liniment and still more sourballs.

When we came to the fork in the road the next time Anna looked so frightened that I felt sorry for her.

"Lisa," she said. "I'm almost sure that I didn't buy any sugar."

"Anna," I said, "don't tell me that you didn't buy the *sugar*. You simply *must* have bought the sugar!"

We squeezed and squeezed the things in Anna's basket, but there was nothing which felt the least bit sugary.

Uncle Emil almost fell across the counter when he saw us again. But he gave us the sugar and still more sourballs.

"I'd better get out a spare jar of sourballs," he said, "because my whole stock is disappearing."

"Don't worry, we won't come back any more," said Anna.

Just before we came to the fork in the road again I said, "Anna, let's *run* past the fork. It's the only way to get by. Otherwise we'll think of something else that we've forgotten."

So we ran by the fork.

"It worked!" said Anna. At last we were on our way home.

"Let's sing a little more," said Anna.

We did. We started with "A piece of Bologna sausage of the best quality," and it sounded just as beautiful and sad as before. Anna said that we ought to introduce that song

at school and sing it at the closing exercises next year. We sang and sang and sang while we struggled up the hill toward Noisy Village.

And then—just as I bellowed, "A piece of Bologna sausage," extra beautifully—Anna took me by the arm and looked absolutely wild.

"Lisa," she said, "we haven't bought any Bologna sausage!"

We sat down by the side of the road and didn't say anything for a long while. Then Anna said that she wished no one had ever invented Bologna sausages.

"Why can't people eat frankfurters instead?" she said.

"We should never have run past the fork in the road," I said.

My, how long the road back seemed this time. We didn't sing any more. Anna said she did not think that song about the Bologna saugage was at all suitable to sing at school.

"No," I said, "not at school and not any other place either. What a ridiculous song!"

When Uncle Emil saw us he held his head, and then he ran to get a new jar of sourballs. But we said that no, thank you, we didn't care for any more sourballs.

"Really?" said Uncle Emil. "What do you want, then?"

"Three pieces of Bologna sausage of the best quality," we said.

"If there *is* such a thing as good Bologna sausage," Anna muttered.

We dragged ourselves homeward. But when we came to the fork in the road Anna looked back and said, "Look, there comes John from the mill, driving his ugly old tawny mare!" John works in a mill that lies on the other side of Noisy Village.

"May we have a ride?" we cried when John had caught up with us.

"Jump right in," said John.

We jumped up on the flour sacks behind John and rode all the way to Noisy Village. I started humming, "A piece of Bologna sausage of the best quality," but Anna said,

"If you sing one more word of that song I'll push you off the wagon."

When I came into the kitchen, Mommy said, "Goodness, Lisa, what a long time you've been gone!"

"No wonder," I said. "With all that Bologna sausage to buy."

When Mommy had taken all the things out of the basket she said, "That was a good girl who remembered everything!"

19 CRAYFISHING AT NOCKEN

DEEP in the forest there is a lake called Nocken. You can't really swim in that lake because the bottom is so muddy, but you can catch crayfish in it. Karl says there is no lake anywhere else in Sweden that is so full of crayfish.

Sometimes Anna says, "Haha, the North Farm Lake is my lake and not yours! You poor thing, you don't have any lake!"

But then I say, "I do so have a lake! Isn't Nocken a lake, may I ask?"

"But it's not your very own lake, because it belongs to everybody in Noisy Village," Anna says. "It's just as much mine as yours. So I really have two lakes!" she says.

Then I get mad and don't play with Anna any more that day. But the next day we decide that it really doesn't matter whose lakes they are, because we can all go swimming in one and catch crayfish in the other.

You aren't allowed to start catching crayfish until August. The day the season starts is almost as much fun as Christmas Eve. Then all of us children go with Daddy and Uncle Nils and Uncle Erik to Nocken. In the evening we set out the crayfish traps in the lake and then we build huts under the trees and sleep there all night. Very, very early the next morning we get up and empty the traps.

Nocken is so far from our village, and the road there is so bad that it's no use to go home and sleep a couple of hours, Daddy says, and so we have to spend the night, and that is the most fun of all.

Every year Mommy says, "I'm so afraid that the children will catch cold."

And Daddy always says, "Oh, nonsense!" He said it this year too when we left. We had a lot to carry—crayfish traps and blankets and rucksacks. And it's a very long way through the forest. But it's no use to whine if you get tired, because Daddy says that no one who whines can come along.

This year, as soon as we got to the lake, we ran to see if there was anything left of our huts from last year. But there wasn't. Britta and Anna and I always have our hut under a large fir tree, where the branches hang down almost to the ground. Daddy and Uncle Erik cut juniper bushes for us to lay around the tree. We leave just one open place where we can crawl in and out. And then we make a thick carpet of fir branches to sleep on.

When we had finished making our hut we went over to
look at the boys'. They always have theirs in a crevice

between two rocks. They put juniper bushes and fir branches over the crevice to make a roof. They have fir branches on the ground to sleep on too.

"It would be nice if we didn't have to have girls around," Karl said when we came. And Bill and Olaf agreed.

"Oh, certainly," Britta said. "But luckily we have a hut that is much nicer to be in than this miserable thing."

Then the boys laughed and said that they felt really sorry for us because we didn't know a thing on earth about building huts. Before we had time to think of a good answer, Uncle Nils called and said we had to come and help mend the crayfish traps. The traps are made of net, and there are always large holes here and there. You can't leave them like that because then the crayfish would crawl out.

We sat on a stone slab down by the lake and mended the traps with string. We talked and had such fun. The sun was beginning to set, and it was very beautiful around the lake and very quiet—except when we were talking, of course.

"Nocken is really a nice lake," Anna said.

Uncle Erik was emptying the water out of the two old rowboats that we keep at Nocken. Uncle Nils and Daddy put bait in the traps. When everything was ready we went out in the rowboats and set out the traps in the water all along the shore.

By the time we had gone around the whole lake it was

getting dark. Anna pinched my arm and said, "It's *almost* more fun than Christmas Eve."

I thought so too. When it was quite dark, Daddy lit a fire on a stone slab as he always does, and we all sat around it and drank hot chocolate and ate sandwiches. The fire shone on the water so that it looked as if it were burning in the lake too. It was very dark and quiet in the forest around us, and Karl said, "I can hear the goblins pattering around in there in the trees."

Anna and I were frightened, but Anna only said, "Don't be silly! There aren't any goblins."

We couldn't help listening anyway, to see if we could hear goblins pattering about in the dark. We couldn't hear anything, though, and we said so to Karl.

"No, of course you can't, because they have hairy feet," he said. "They sneak about very quietly and then stand behind the trees and stare at us."

"I don't believe a word of it," I said and moved a little closer to Anna.

"It's true enough," Karl said. "The whole forest is full of goblins' eyes that are staring at us right now. But they don't dare come here because they're afraid of our fire."

Then Daddy told Karl to stop telling the little girls things that weren't true. He put more branches on the fire and it flared up and shone beautifully. I didn't *think* there were any goblins, but just to be sure I climbed up in Daddy's lap, and Anna went over and sat in Uncle Erik's lap. Then

Uncle Erik whistled for us. He can whistle like a bird if he wants to.

I thought that if there really were goblins in the forest they'd surely wonder why we were sitting there around a fire and listening to Uncle Erik whistling away in the middle of the night.

Uncle Nils and Daddy and Uncle Erik told stories too. We laughed because they were such funny stories. The boys took their flashlights down to the edge of the water to look for crayfish. They found twenty-three and put them in a tin can.

Karl said to Bill and Olaf, "If the girls are good and act like human beings, we'll invite them to a crayfish party tomorrow night."

"Yes, but of course it all depends on how they behave," Bill said.

"It'll have to be an awfully good behavior," Olaf said.

When the fire had almost burned down, Uncle Erik said that it was time to go to sleep. The daddies didn't have a hut but just rolled themselves up in their blankets and slept around the fire. Britta and Anna and I crept down under our wonderful fir tree and rolled up in blankets too. We were just going to sleep when we heard something pattering outside. I cried, "Who is it?"

"A goblin," Karl said in the most gruesome voice. We looked out through the opening between the juniper bushes, and there stood the boys with their flashlights. They said they wanted to see our hut, so they crept in, one at a time. There was room for all of us, although it was a little crowded. The boys said that our hut was fairly decent, after all—but not as nice as theirs, of course. Then they crept out again and Karl said, "This is a pretty good hut, but of course it's not goblin-proof!"

The boys left and we tried to go to sleep. First we talked a little, but it feels so funny when you lie in the woods at night and talk. It feels as if someone were standing outside in the dark listening.

I think Britta and Anna went to sleep long before I did. I lay awake and listened to the rustling of the forest. There was just a little rustling, and small waves lapped against the shore very quietly. It felt strange and all of a sudden I didn't know whether I was happy or sad. I lay there and tried to decide, but I couldn't. Perhaps you get a little funny from sleeping in the woods.

Daddy came and woke us up at four in the morning. We shivered with cold but were very happy. The sun was shining, and we crept out of our hut and swung our arms back and forth to get warm. Then Daddy gave us hot chocolate. There was a bit of fog over the lake, but it soon went away, and we took the rowboats out to pick up the crayfish traps.

I feel sorry for all people who have never rowed out on a lake at four in the morning and picked up crayfish traps.

There were lots of crayfish in nearly all the traps. Karl and Bill will take hold of crayfish any old way, but I won't. Bill took out one crayfish and sat looking at her for a while. Then all of a sudden he let her go in the lake.

"Are you nuts!" Karl cried. "Throwing crayfish back into the lake!"

"She had such sad eyes," Bill said.

"My, but you're stupid," Karl said. "Now I bet she'll swim all over the lake and tattle to the other crayfish that we're here. Then we won't get any more this year. What did you have to do that for?"

"She had such sad eyes," Bill said again.

But just then we met the other boat and we yelled to Olaf and Britta and Anna, "Have you got a lot of crayfish?"

"Almost the whole boat full," Olaf yelled.

Then we rowed to our camping place and emptied all the crayfish into two large clothes baskets with lids. We packed everything we had at the camp and started to walk toward home. There was dew in the grass, and there were spiderwebs here and there and they sparkled like diamonds. My feet were wet, and I was sleepy and hungry. I was also very, very happy, because it was such fun to walk in a long row on the path and bring home so many crayfish. Uncle Erik whistled and we sang:

"A hunter did a-hunting—go
Among the leaves so green—O."

Suddenly Karl cried, "I see the smoke from Noisy Village!"

And then we all saw the smoke from three chimneys rising above the trees and we knew that they were awake at North Farm and Middle Farm and South Farm. When we had gone a little farther we could see all of Noisy Village. The sun was shining on the windows of the houses, and they looked beautiful.

"I feel sorry for people who don't have any place to live," I said to Anna.

"*I* feel sorry for people who don't live in Noisy Village," Anna said.